This book belongs to

....

and I wish for

....

....

Hi! We're the Wish sisters!

I'm Flick and this is my little sister, Birdie.

We're not the Wish sisters because it's our last name, but because there's so much wishing in our house.

'Gah!'

It all started when our Granny Aggie found an imp in an old bottle and wished for us to have unlimited wishes!

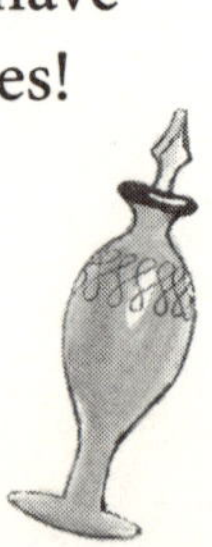

You'd think having unlimited wishes would be fun. And it is! It's also a whole lot of trouble.

**'My name is Imp,
not he or she,
just a plain old imp
I be.'**

The imp likes to twist wishes and make them go wrong. It twisted Granny Aggie's wish so that only Birdie can wish.

Now I really have to be the best big sister ever to help keep Birdie's wishes under control!

The Wish Sisters

The Running Wish

Allison Rushby

illustrated by Karen Blair

UQP

1

Green team

'How do I look?'

Flick's dad entered the kitchen and did a twirl.

Flick was sitting at the kitchen bench with her best friend, Oli. They both took in Flick's dad's outfit. He was wearing green-and-black stripy socks, black shorts, a green tulle skirt and a green t-shirt.

He had even sprayed his hair green.

Flick and Oli were wearing green t-shirts too. Today was their school's sports day and they were both in the green team.

'Green enough?' Flick's dad struck a pose.

Flick's dad always got very excited about sports day. Maybe too excited.

'Definitely green enough,' Flick and Oli said at the same time.

Flick's little sister, Birdie, looked up. She was playing with her blocks on the floor. She was wearing a white onesie with tiny green polka dots on it. This was the greenest outfit Birdie had.

'Gah!' she said.

‘That’s right, Birdie. Trophy,’ Flick’s dad said. ‘This is going to be my year. I can feel it. I’ve been training.’ He stretched his legs.

Flick frowned. Her dad hadn’t really been training. He had just gone on two runs last week. Every year he tried to win the parent–teacher race. And every year Ms Pawar, one of the teachers, would beat him.

Flick’s dad did a little warm-up jog. ‘Oh! I’ve just had a thought. I’ve got a pair of big green party glasses somewhere.’ He darted out of the room.

Flick and Oli glanced at one another.

‘Ms Pawar just did a triathlon,’ Oli said.

'I don't think your dad is going to win. Unless Birdie …' He looked over at Flick's little sister.

Hearing her name, Birdie looked up.

'Shhh!' Flick said to Oli. 'Don't give Birdie any **W-I-S-H-I-N-G** ideas.'

There'd been a lot of wishing going on at Flick's house lately. This was because Flick's Granny Aggie had left her grandbabies (that was Flick and Birdie) an imp in a bottle. The imp could grant unlimited wishes! But, as it turned out, imps were tricksy creatures. The imp had twisted Granny Aggie's wish. The imp said Granny Aggie had given her wishes to her grand*babies* not grand*children*, and because Flick wasn't a baby, she couldn't wish!

Since Birdie had discovered she could wish, a lot of strange things had been happening. Birdie had wished for parties with marshmallow pits and rainbow slides made out of sour straps and unicorns that pooped cupcakes. She had wished for a litter of puppies to jump out of an advertisement. And she had wished to be as big as Flick.

Flick was a bit worried about what Birdie might wish for at the school sports day.

Flick's parents had been worried too.

'She could wish for anything!' Flick's mum had said last night, when Birdie was in bed. 'And I'll be at work, so I won't be able to help.'

'That's true,' Flick's dad had replied. 'But we have to go. I have to run in my race.'

In the end, they had decided to cross their fingers and hope it would be okay. During the day, Flick and her dad would remind Birdie that sports day was a wish-free zone. And Flick's mum would stop by on her lunch break to see if everything was going okay.

Flick went over to Birdie and got down on the floor with her.

'Gah!' Birdie said. She passed Flick a block.

‘Thanks, Birdie,’ Flick said. She put the block on top of the pile Birdie had in front of her.

Birdie pushed the pile over and laughed, clapping her hands.

‘Um, Birdie?’ Flick got her sister’s attention.

Birdie looked up.

‘Just remember. No wishes today. Okay?’

Birdie held her sister’s gaze for a moment. ‘Bleh.’ Birdie turned away and went back to her blocks.

Flick got up from the floor. ‘I think Birdie’s getting a bit sick of being lectured about wishing,’ she said to Oli.

'If I were you, I'd stop worrying about wishing and start worrying about running,' Oli said. 'Come on, we've still got a few minutes before we have to go. Let's go outside and practise a bit more.'

2

PARP!

'PARP!' Oli made a funny noise.

Instead of running, Flick opened her eyes. She started to laugh. Sitting on the grass in the backyard, Birdie laughed too.

'*Parp?*' Flick asked.

Oli put his hands on his hips. 'Well, what sort of noise do *you* think an air horn makes?'

Flick thought about this. 'Okay, I guess it does sound a bit like *parp*. Sorry, Oli, it just sounded funny.'

Now Oli laughed too. 'It did a bit.'

Flick was glad Oli seemed happy today. Last week, Oli had fallen over in the playground. He had cut his leg on a rock and had needed five stitches. He could walk fine, but it still hurt a bit to run, so he wasn't able to compete in any of the races at the sports day.

This was bad news for Oli, but also bad news for the green team. Oli was the green team's best runner in year three. They had been counting on Oli to win some points in his race. This was because the green team was hoping to win the sports day cup. They had come close last year. They had come close the year before too. The green team needed every point they could get.

Izzy was a fast swimmer, but not a fast runner. Yusuf had a broken wrist and couldn't run today. Minh said she would run her hardest, but that Flick was green team's best chance, because she was faster.

This was true. Flick was a faster runner than Minh when she got going. But Flick also had a problem. A starting problem.

The problem was that Flick always worried about starting the race too early. She didn't want to start running too soon because she knew she could get disqualified. So Flick always waited for the air horn noise. Then she checked that everyone else had started running. And then she ran.

This was not a good way to win a race.

Oli had told Ms Pawar about Flick's problem. Ms Pawar had been really nice and let them practise with the air horn at lunchtime. Oli had even come up with a trick Flick could use. She had to close her eyes before the start of the race. Then, as soon as she heard the air horn, she had to start running.

This way, Flick didn't worry about what anyone else was doing. She just listened for the air horn. And *then* she ran.

'I wish we had an air horn,' Oli said.

'Oli!' Flick gasped.

Oli realised what he'd said. 'Oops! Sorry!'

But it was too late.

'Gah, gah, gah!' Birdie said.

Someone appeared beside Birdie on the grass.

The someone opened its mouth and the exact loud noise the air horn made exited it. ***'PARP!'***

The someone had tightly curled, light purple hair. Hoofed legs. Stubby horns. Pointed ears. And a cheeky, gap-toothed grin.

It was the imp.

'PARP!' the imp said again.

Birdie laughed and clapped her hands. ***'PARP!'*** The air horn noise came out of her mouth too. ***'PARP!'***

Flick looked at Oli with wide eyes. How could such a big noise come out of such a little baby?

Oli looked around. And then he shrugged.

'I say we go for it,' he said. 'No one's watching. Are you ready, Flick? Close your eyes and pretend it's the big race. I'll give Birdie the signal.'

Flick supposed he was right. She took her place and closed her eyes. She waited, listening. Ready to take off the moment she heard the …

'PARP!'

Flick burst off, opening her eyes as she went. She ran a short distance and then turned back.

'Perfect timing, Flick!' Oli clapped.

'PARP!' Birdie said again. She looked at the imp. ***'PARP, PARP, PARP!'*** She coughed a bit, like the *parp*ing was hurting her throat. Then, **'Gah!'** Her voice changed back again. Birdie had unwished her wish. She had obviously had enough of being an air horn.

The imp stood and then stomped a hoof. 'Ugh. You're just no fun!' It disappeared with a huff.

'Ready, green team?' Flick's dad called out from the house.

Flick wasn't sure she was ready. As she picked up her little sister, Flick wondered if a wish could help with her race. Not to make her faster, or to win, but just so she started at the right time. But, no. She couldn't. That wouldn't be fair. And anyway, the imp liked to twist wishes.

Flick knew if Birdie made a wish for Flick to start quickly, it would backfire somehow. She would end up bursting off like a rocket before slowing down to a snail's pace. Or she'd run really fast, but on the spot.

Flick took a deep breath. She could do this. And it was better to do this on her own.

3

The first thing to go wrong

On the walk to school, Flick thought a lot about the wishes. Birdie becoming an air horn this morning had been useful and fun, but Flick knew they needed to be careful. You never knew what Birdie might wish for. Birdie seemed to get wishing ideas from anywhere and everywhere. Especially when she was excited.

And sports day was sure to be exciting.

Flick also knew that they had been lucky Mrs Mortlake hadn't heard Birdie *parp*ing. Mrs Mortlake was their next-door neighbour. She wasn't a bad person, she was just nosy. She always wanted to know what everyone on Honeysuckle Street was up to. She even had a little stool beside her fence so she could see into Flick's family's backyard! She often liked to mention her niece: 'She's a television news reporter, you know!' If Mrs Mortlake found out about the wishes, the whole world would know.

Flick breathed a sigh of relief when they were past Mrs Mortlake's house.

Flick's dad stopped at the traffic lights and pressed the button so they could cross the road. A man leaned out of a car window. He stared at Flick's dad's green outfit. 'When are the other aliens coming?' he called out.

Flick's dad laughed. 'Aliens! Ha! I guess we are all looking a bit green.'

Birdie laughed too. 'Gah!' she said. **'Gah, gah, gah!'**

But Flick's mind was racing. 'Dad!' she said as they all crossed the road. 'We have to be careful! What if Birdie wished for A-L-I-E-N-S?' She spelled the word out.

'Ooohhhh … I didn't think of that,' Flick's dad said. When they got to the other side of the road, he stopped and crouched down beside Birdie. 'Oh!' he said in surprise.

Flick peered into the stroller. 'Birdie!' she yelped. Her sister was green! She was green from head to toe! Birdie had green skin, green hair, green teeth. Even the whites of her eyes were pale green. Flick guessed her little sister had wished for a green outfit.

A purple hand waved from the stroller basket.

'Go, green team!' the imp called out in a singsong voice.

Flick ducked down to look in the stroller basket. 'I think you'd better be careful today,' she told the imp. 'There will be lots of adults at sports day. And you're always saying adults are trouble.'

The imp had warned them lots of times not to let adults know about the wishes. The imp had told them that adults would want the wishes for themselves and only wished for boring things like money.

'I guess you're saying I should stay in the stroller basket,' the imp said.

'You shouldn't even be here at all!' Flick replied.

Birdie was busy inspecting her arms and legs. Her face scrunched up. It didn't look like she was enjoying her new green body. 'Bleh!' she said. **'Bleh, bleh, bleh.'**

In the blink of an eye, Birdie was back to her normal self.

Flick's dad pulled Birdie's stroller off the footpath. 'Right,' he said. 'I think we need to have a little talk. I think it would be good if, for just one day, we could pretend there are no wishes.' He then gave Birdie another big lecture about wishing.

When he was done, Birdie blew a raspberry. A big one. **'Bleh, bleh, bleh.'** Birdie was definitely tired of being lectured.

Oli bent down and looked in the stroller basket. 'I think the imp's gone off in a huff again.'

Flick's dad stood. 'Hmmm? Sorry?'

'I think Birdie understood what you meant about the wishes,' Oli said.

'What wishes?' Flick's dad replied.

4

The second thing to go wrong

Oli and Flick looked at each other in confusion. And then Oli grinned. 'Ah, I get it!'

'You do?' Flick said.

'Yep,' Oli replied. 'We're really going to do it. We're all going to pretend we don't know anything about wishes. We're all just going to act like this is a normal sports day.'

‘It is a normal sports day,’ Flick’s dad said as they started off again towards school.

‘I hope so!’ Flick said. This was actually a pretty good idea. Maybe if they stopped focusing on the wishes, Birdie wouldn’t make any. Maybe Birdie would start to think it was just a normal sports day too. Flick decided she should play along and changed the subject. ‘What do you think the surprise is going to be?’ she asked Oli.

The principal, Ms Lee, had told the school at assembly that there would be a special surprise at sports day. Everyone was eager to find out what it would be.

Oli grinned. 'I think it's going to be a snow cone machine.'

'That would be amazing!' Flick said excitedly. But then her eyes flicked to Birdie. They might not be talking about wishes, but she still didn't want Birdie getting any ideas.

'Oops, sorry.' Oli saw Flick looking at her little sister. 'Though I'm not sure what could go wrong with snow cones,' he whispered.

'I can,' Flick whispered back. 'The whole sports field could be covered with crushed ice. We'd all be slipping and sliding. It would be like the Winter Olympics.'

They looked at each other and laughed.

Maybe that wouldn't be such a bad wish. It sounded like fun.

'In you go.' Flick's dad opened the school oval's metal gate. Already the field was a riot of colour. The green team, red team, blue team and yellow team were all setting up in their zones. Excited voices carried across the grass. Banners, streamers and bunting fluttered in the breeze.

Flick, Oli, Flick's dad and Birdie made their way over to the green team's tent. Everyone loved Flick's dad's outfit and lots of people said they couldn't wait for the parent–teacher race.

RED RULES
BLUE IS BEST
YELL FOR YELLOW!
GREEN TEAM
GO, GO, GO GREEN!

It was going to be a great day.

Until it wasn't.

'Um, Flick?' Oli said. He grabbed Flick's arm. 'I think I might know what the surprise is.'

Flick turned to see Oli pointing at something. The trophy table.

Standing in front of it was the principal, Ms Lee.

And Mrs Mortlake.

And a news crew.

5

The Busybodies

'What's Mrs Mortlake doing here?' Oli said.

Flick saw a few other adults she knew, including nice Mr Tran, who also lived on Honeysuckle Street. 'Oh, no!' she groaned. 'It's the Busybodies.'

The Busybodies were a community group. You had to be over sixty years old to join. They were all about keeping older people active. There were walking groups and bus tours and a community garden and all sorts of activities. Mr Tran was the president and Mrs Mortlake was the vice-president. Apparently, Mrs Mortlake was always trying to be the president, but everyone liked Mr Tran too much.

Flick's mum and dad thought the Busybodies was the funniest name ever. Flick's mum always said they 'hadn't thought the name through'.

Flick thought maybe they had thought it through. After all, Mrs Mortlake did have that special stool she used to look over the fence into Flick's family's back garden.

'The Busybodies must be handing out the trophies and ribbons today,' Flick's dad said. 'And that's exciting about the news crew! Maybe they'll catch my winning moment on camera.'

'You're not worried?' Flick asked.

'No. Because I've been training!' Flick's dad said.

Flick gave him a look. 'I mean about the news crew. And the **W-I-S-H-E-S,**' she said.

'What wishes?'

'Flick!' Oli said. 'You've got to play along, remember?'

'I think they're about to start marking the roll,' Flick's dad told them. 'You'd better go find your teacher. I'll give Birdie her snack.'

Flick watched as her dad pushed Birdie's stroller off to a corner of the tent. She couldn't believe he was pleased to see the news crew!

And Mrs Mortlake!

Flick and Oli went and got marked off the roll. Then they went to look at the big board with all the events listed on it.

'There you are.' Oli pointed at Flick's name.

Flick gulped. There she was. She would be running in the fourth race of the day.

'Don't worry,' Oli said. 'Just remember to use your secret weapon! Just like this morning.'

Flick nodded. 'There's Dad's race.' Flick pointed to the parent–teacher race. It was just before lunch. 'Ms Pawar's definitely running today.'

'Maybe he'll come second?' Oli suggested.

'Everyone gather around!' one of the teachers called out. 'Ms Lee is going to say a few words. Then we'll get started.'

6

Let the races begin

Ms Lee did an Acknowledgement of Country and welcomed the parents and guardians. Then she challenged all the teams to see who could cheer the loudest.

'And I'd like to hear the biggest cheer of all for the Busybodies,' she said, 'who've kindly offered to help out with the trophies and ribbons today. The Busybodies have also invited a news crew to film a segment on keeping active, no matter what age you are. I'm sure you'll all be very excited to see yourselves on television tonight.'

Flick and Oli looked at one another in alarm. Flick knew Oli was thinking the same thing she was. What if Birdie turned green again? What if she *parp*ed?

They turned back to see Mrs Mortlake stepping in front of Ms Lee to use the microphone.

'Yes, that's right, Ms Lee. I'm very happy to have invited the news crew today.'

Oli nudged Flick. 'She's not even the president!' he whispered. 'Mr Tran should be speaking!'

Ms Lee took the microphone out of its stand before Mrs Mortlake could continue. 'Thank you, Mrs Mortlake and the Busybodies.'

Mr Tran walked over to Mrs Mortlake. He spoke quietly to her. It appeared he needed her for important Busybodies business at the trophy table.

Flick eyed the news crew warily. Then she turned to see what Birdie and her dad were up to. She spotted them standing in the shade just inside the green team tent.

'Hey, look at Birdie!' she said to Oli.

Birdie was asleep.

Parp! Someone tested the air horn, making both Oli and Flick jump.

They looked at each other and laughed. For a second, they had thought it was Birdie making the noise! But she was still sound asleep.

Flick couldn't believe her luck.

The day was warm. There was a nice cool breeze. And Birdie had been asleep all morning.

Birdie napped through the high jump. And through the long jump. And through the shot-put. Birdie even napped through the first few races.

'Do you think I should wake Birdie up?' Flick's dad asked as Flick got ready for her race. 'We don't want her to miss you running.'

Flick shook her head hard. 'No! If you wake her up, she'll just be cranky.'

'Okay, then. Good luck!'

Oli walked Flick over to the starting line.

Flick gulped. Ava from the red team was there. She was fast. So was Eli from the yellow team.

'Don't worry about everyone else. Just remember what you have to do,' Oli told her.

Flick nodded. Oli was right. She could do this. She'd done it this morning.

'You might even enjoy it,' Oli said.

'Running is actually pretty fun. Just close your eyes. Wait for the air horn. And then run, run, run. You don't even need to worry about Birdie wishing for something.'

Flick glanced over at Birdie. She was still asleep in her stroller. Flick's dad saw her looking and waved. Flick waved back. And then she grinned. Suddenly, she felt a lot more positive about sports day. The sky was blue. The bunting was flapping in the breeze. And she was surrounded by her school friends.

Flick took her place.

She closed her eyes.

And then the air horn went.

7

Run, run, run

Flick took off as fast as she could go. She opened her eyes and she ran, ran, ran. She didn't worry about the other runners. She just stuck to her lane and ran her own race. And the funny thing was, before she knew it, she was nearing the finish line.

Eli came first.

Flick came second.

And Ava came third.

Flick couldn't believe it.

She had won five whole points for the green team!

Flick shook hands with all the other runners and received her ribbon from Mr Tran.

'Great work, Flick!' Mr Tran said.

Flick was then swept up by the green team who jumped about, celebrating.

'I knew you could do it!' Oli cheered.

'That was actually fun!' Flick said, still in a daze.

Flick's dad came over to take a photo. 'Second place, Flick! I never knew you could run so fast!'

'Me either!' Flick said. 'But I can. Well, thanks to Oli's trick.'

Oli shook his head. 'No way. You did it all by yourself.' He lowered his voice so only Flick and her dad could hear. 'You didn't even need any help from the **W-I-S-H-E-S.**'

'Why are you talking about wishes again?' Flick's dad asked.

Flick and Oli looked up at him. Behind his large green party glasses, his face looked sort of ... blank.

And that's when they realised. Flick's dad wasn't playing a game.

He truly didn't know about the wishes.

It was just like Flick had thought.

Birdie was sick of being lectured about wishes.

So Birdie had made their dad forget.

The air horn *parp*ed again, signalling the start of the next race.

In her stroller, Birdie stirred. She yawned. Then stretched her arms.

'Ah! All rested!' Flick's dad said. He bent down and picked Birdie up. 'Come on, then. We'll go change your nappy. And then we might do some warm-up exercises for the big race.'

Birdie clapped her hands. 'Gah!' she said, looking excited. She waved to all the green team members as her dad carried her off.

Flick and Oli returned to the green team tent.

'I can't believe Birdie made your dad forget about the wishes!' Oli said.

'I can,' Flick groaned. 'We've already had Birdie become an air horn and turn green today. I can't imagine what she'll wish for next. And Dad can't do anything about it!'

'Do you think your mum will get here soon?' Oli asked.

'I don't think she'll get here before Dad's race,' Flick said.

Flick's dad returned to the green team

tent a few minutes later. He gave Birdie some sandwiches. And then he started doing a whole lot of stretches.

After a while, he picked Birdie up and pretended that she was doing stretches too. Birdie clapped and laughed.

Flick and Oli watched as Flick's dad danced around with Birdie chanting, 'Green team, green team!'

'Gah, gah!' Birdie called out, getting more and more excited. 'Gah, gah!'

Flick and Oli looked at one another nervously. They sensed a wish coming up.

Very soon.

8

Bicycle legs

Flick's dad was taking his warm-up very seriously.

He had set up a picnic rug in a corner of the tent and was doing some complicated stretches on it. Birdie sat on a corner of the rug, her stroller by her side.

'Yoo-hoo! Oh, yoo-hoo!'

Mrs Mortlake entered the tent. She had

someone with her. A woman in a suit. 'Ah, there you are!' Mrs Mortlake approached Flick's dad. 'I was telling my niece you're just the person we need.'

'I am?' Flick's dad kept stretching.

'Yes. She needs to interview a parent before the big race. She's a news reporter, you know.'

'I love your costume,' Mrs Mortlake's niece said. 'Would you mind if I grabbed the news crew? They're just outside.'

'Not at all!' Flick's dad said. 'I'll finish up with some bicycle legs and be right with you.'

'Thank you!' Mrs Mortlake's niece said. She and Mrs Mortlake left.

Flick's dad sat down on the rug.

'Right. Time for bicycle legs. Birdie, do you want to do some too?'

'Gah!' Birdie definitely wanted to do bicycle legs.

Flick's dad popped Birdie onto her back and then lay down beside her. He put his legs up in the air and began to pedal. Birdie did her best to copy him, laughing.

'Faster, Birdie! Faster!' Flick's dad said.

Birdie laughed harder. She thought bicycle legs were the funniest thing ever.

Flick's dad laughed too. 'You can go faster than that!'

'Gah, gah, gah!' Birdie said.

Flick was taking a bite of her muesli bar when it happened.

Birdie's legs began to spin faster. And faster.

So did her dad's.

They started spinning so fast they were a blur!

'All that training's paid off!' Flick's dad huffed.

Flick grabbed Oli. 'We need to hide them while we sort this out!' she said.

They looked about. And then Oli spotted something. 'Quick, grab that banner,' he said.

Oli was pointing at a Busybodies banner that was set up outside their tent.

It was next to a table with some Busybodies leaflets on it.

Flick sped out to the table. Mr Tran was there, handing out leaflets.

'Can-I-just-borrow-your-banner-for-a-minute-please?' Flick said in a rush, already tugging the stakes out of the ground.

'Sure,' Mr Tran said, looking confused.

'Thanks, Mr Tran!' Flick ran off.

Back inside the tent, she got Oli to hold the banner so no one would be able to see her dad and Birdie. And then Flick dived for the stroller basket. The imp was hanging out in there, watching Birdie and Flick's dad. When it saw Flick, it did that snorty laugh it often did.

‘Imagine if your dad went this fast in the race!’ the imp said. ‘It would be awesome!’

‘It would not be awesome,’ Flick said. ‘It would be unfair.’

‘And awesome!’ The imp snort-laughed again.

‘You have to make them stop,’ Flick said urgently. ‘The news crew is coming.’

‘Can’t.’ The imp shrugged.

Flick knew this was true. Only Birdie could unwish the wish.

‘Birdie!’ Flick got down beside her sister and her super-fast legs. ‘You have to stop the bicycle legs! Mrs Mortlake’s coming back with the news crew.’

Birdie looked at her big sister. Then she blew a raspberry. She was having fun doing super-fast bicycle legs.

Flick looked to her dad for help. But then she remembered he couldn't help. Birdie had made him forget about the wishes!

'Do you need help with that banner?'

It was Mr Tran.

'Goodness, they are fast, aren't they?' he said, watching Flick's dad and Birdie for a moment. 'Look at those legs go!'

Flick stared up at Mr Tran. Couldn't he see that legs simply didn't go that fast?

But there was no time to think about this. Flick bent down again and whispered to her sister, 'Birdie, you have to stop.

Right now! If everyone finds out, they'll want to take your wishes away. Also, I think you've worn poor Dad out!'

Birdie glanced over at their dad. He was pretty red in the face now.

'Gah!' Birdie said.

And, just like that, the bicycle legs stopped.

The sound of a raspberry came from the stroller basket.

Slowly, Flick looked back up at Mr Tran.

'All done with the banner?' he asked. 'I'll take it back if you don't need it anymore.'

Oli handed it to him.

And then, with a wink, Mr Tran was gone.

Flick froze in shock. Mr Tran had acted like the super-fast bicycle legs were completely normal. There had been other wishes in the past that Mr Tran hadn't been very surprised about too. Mr Tran had been a good friend of Granny Aggie's. Flick was starting to wonder just how much he knew …

'Phew! I didn't know I had that in me!' Flick's dad said. He stood as the news crew approached. 'I hope I have enough energy left for this interview. And for the big race!'

9

At the starting line

Flick's dad did a quick interview with the news crew. He explained how important fitness was and how much he'd been training for the big race. Mrs Mortlake had a lot to say, of course.

'It's so important to keep healthy,' she said right into the camera. 'You don't need to spend a lot of money. Just move!

The Busybodies are all about keeping active. And keeping active starts with the youth of today.'

'Thank you, Mrs Mortlake, president of the Busybodies,' Mrs Mortlake's news reporter niece said.

Mrs Mortlake cleared her throat. 'Yes, well. *Vice*-president.'

The interview ended just in time – Ms Lee announced over the loudspeaker that the parent–teacher race would be starting in five minutes.

'We'd best get you to the starting line!' Mrs Mortlake began to shuffle Flick's dad out of the tent. Flick and Oli followed close behind with Birdie.

'What a shame your mother will miss the race,' Mrs Mortlake said to Flick as they walked.

'I think there must be traffic,' Flick's dad replied. 'Maybe we should ask your news crew if we can use the traffic helicopter to fly her in? Wouldn't that be great, kids? There's plenty of room to land a helicopter right here on the field.' He laughed heartily.

'Gah!' Birdie laughed too. She seemed to think that would be a great idea.

Flick and Oli shared a nervous look.

And then they heard a noise.

Wait. Was that ...?

It was!

Flick could hear the whirring sound of a helicopter's blades. The group all looked up at the sky.

Flick's dad laughed again. 'What a coincidence. That must be her now!'

Flick's mouth fell open. How would they ever explain her mum being helicoptered into the school sports day!

Birdie pointed at the helicopter. 'Gah!' she said.

The helicopter flew right over them.

'Yes, that's right, Birdie. Helicopter,' Flick's dad said.

Flick breathed a

sigh of relief. It was just a coincidence. The helicopter wasn't a wish!

'Well, I'd best be off.'

'Good luck, Dad!' Flick said.

The green team were all heading over to the racetrack now. Flick, Oli and Birdie joined them. They got a great spot near the finish line.

All the teams began to whoop and cheer as the runners lined up.

'Green team, green team, green team!' the green team chanted.

'Gah gah, gah gah, gah gah!' Birdie clearly couldn't wait for the race to start.

'Birdie is getting into this!' Oli said. 'I think she really wants your dad to win.'

'That's what I'm afraid of,' Flick replied.

At the starting line, Flick's dad had taken his place. There were three other parents and four teachers. Flick's dad was standing right beside Ms Pawar, in her yellow team outfit.

Flick whispered in her little sister's ear, 'Birdie, no wishes about the race, okay? It wouldn't be fair.' Flick knew her Granny Aggie would never have wanted them to use the wishes for something like that.

'Gah,' Birdie said, her eyes on the starting line.

'Birdie?' Flick tried again.

Birdie glanced at her big sister. 'Gah!' She looked a bit cross.

Flick really hoped she'd understood.

Parp! sounded the air horn.

The race had begun.

10

The big race

The four parents and four teachers took off. The race was only two hundred metres and it didn't take long to see who stood a chance of winning. Several runners quickly fell behind. Flick's dad, Ms Pawar and the new PE teacher, Mr Hoskins, were the fastest.

One hundred metres down, Mr

Hoskins was in front. Flick's dad and Ms Pawar were close behind.

On the sidelines, all the teams were jumping about. They cheered and whooped for their runners.

'Come on, Dad!' Flick yelled. The runners were closing in on the finish line now.

'Gah!' Birdie yelled too. She waved her little hands.

Suddenly, Ms Pawar made a break for it. She pumped her arms harder and began to pull out further in front. Now she was almost even with Mr Hoskins. Flick's dad was going to come in third.

Flick's dad glanced sideways. It was

now or never. He pumped his arms harder too.

The finish line was so close!

And that's when it happened.

A string of brightly coloured bunting hung above the finish line. As the runners approached, a strong breeze gusted across the field, knocking the bunting loose. It flew away, landing across Mr Hoskins's eyes. He staggered and fell, rolling on the ground.

The end of the bunting wrapped around Ms Pawar's legs. She swayed, grabbing the person beside her – Flick's dad. He tried to steady Ms Pawar, but lost his balance. Ms Pawar fell to the ground, tripping Flick's dad as she went.

Flick's dad stumbled. He took one, two, three wobbly steps and then landed flat on his face.

Across the finish line.

The crowd gasped.

Mr Hoskins, Ms Pawar and Flick's dad all righted themselves. People rushed over to help. Luckily, it seemed they were all okay. Mr Hoskins and Ms Pawar crossed the finish line and everyone clapped. No one had been hurt!

In fact, Ms Pawar and Mr Hoskins seemed to think the whole thing was hilarious. They were howling with laughter!

RED RULES
GO, GO, GO

But was Flick's dad the winner? No one was really sure.

The officials all put their heads together.

And then the announcement came over the loudspeaker. The green team parent had won the parent–teacher race.

The green team went wild!

Ms Pawar and Mr Hoskins were still laughing. They congratulated Flick's dad, who had started laughing too.

But Flick … Flick didn't laugh. Flick stayed very, very still and stared at Birdie.

Because she knew that Birdie had made a wish.

Birdie had wished for their dad to win the race.

'That was unbelievable!' Oli laughed.

'Exactly,' Flick said. She was furious.

'Ohhh …' Oli said, realising what had happened. 'Oh.'

'Yes. Oh,' Flick said. She looked at her dad, who was still jumping about. If he knew what Birdie had done, he would have been so cross. He never would have wanted to win by cheating.

Flick's mum appeared. 'I made it just in time. What a race! What an ending! I couldn't believe my eyes.'

'Me either.' Flick handed Birdie to her mother. She could barely look at her sister.

Flick's dad bounded over. 'How about that!'

‘Gah, gah, gah!’ Birdie said.

‘I’ll say, Birdie!’ Flick’s dad said. But then, ‘Oh my goodness!’ he exclaimed as he stared at his youngest daughter.

Flick and Oli followed his gaze until they saw what he was looking at.

And what he was looking at was yet another wish.

11

Winner winner, chicken dinner

This wish was a t-shirt.

'You guys!' Flick's dad said. 'I can't believe you made a t-shirt! You believed in me all along! You even guessed exactly what I'd wear!'

Birdie's t-shirt had a cartoon picture of their dad on it. He was dressed in green-and-black stripy socks, black shorts, a green tulle skirt and a green t-shirt. The cartoon dad even had green hair. And he was holding a trophy!

'Gah!' Birdie looked very pleased with herself.

'Come over with me for the trophy presentation!' Flick's dad said to Flick.

'No, thanks,' Flick said.

'Gah!' Birdie was keen to go with her dad. She pointed to all the shiny trophies.

'Are you sure you don't want to come with us?' Flick's dad asked.

Flick nodded.

'Well, all right, then.' He took Birdie from Flick's mum and headed over to the table.

Flick watched from afar as her dad received his trophy. The worst bit was seeing how happy he was. Because if he knew the truth – that he'd won because of a wish – he wouldn't be happy at all. He'd have given the trophy back and made everyone re-run the race.

Over at the trophy table, the green team gathered. The parents took lots of photos. Flick's mum had gone over to take photos too.

'We'd better join them,' Oli told Flick.

Flick didn't want to, but she knew it would look strange if they didn't.

She made herself walk over. And she forced herself to smile in the photos.

After the photos were all done, Flick's mum looked at her watch. 'We'd best go and have a bite to eat,' she said. 'With all the traffic, I'll have to turn around and go back to work shortly.'

Flick's dad led the way across the field and back to the green team's tent. Flick managed to pull her mother to one side as they walked. 'Birdie's done something terrible,' she said so that only her mum and Oli could hear. 'Actually, she's done two terrible things.'

'What did she do?' her mum asked.

'She made Dad forget about the wishes. And she wished for him to win the parent–teacher race.'

'Wishes? What wishes?' Flick's mum said, confused.

Flick and Oli exchanged horrified glances. Oh, no! Birdie had made *both* her parents forget.

'Oh,' Flick answered her mother. 'Don't worry. It was … just a joke.'

'If you say so!' Flick's mum said.

Flick stayed back with Oli as her mum went on ahead. 'This is bad. So bad! What if Birdie makes me forget too? Or both of us? And then she keeps wishing? She could wish for anything the way she's going today!'

Oli nodded. 'And the news crew would film it.'

'And it would be on TV. On the internet. *Everywhere!*'

The pair imagined just how bad this could be. How people might try to take advantage of Birdie being small. How they might try to make the wishes their own. Flick thought of another t-shirt then. A special one she had at home. Her Granny Aggie had given it to her. The front of the t-shirt said, *Best Big Sister Ever.* Flick loved that t-shirt. When Granny Aggie had given it to her, Flick had made a silent promise to try to be the best big sister ever. She was really angry with Birdie for wishing for their dad to win the race. And for making Mum and Dad forget about the wishes.

But she also had to protect her little sister.

'What do you think we should do?' Oli asked.

Flick thought for a moment. 'I guess … all we can really do is speak to Birdie.' She raced up to her dad and took Birdie from him. Then she waited for her parents to go on ahead.

'Birdie,' Flick began when they were out of earshot. 'We know you've made Mum and Dad forget about the wishes.'

'Gah,' Birdie said.

'You have to unwish that wish, Birdie!' Flick told her sternly.

Birdie blew a raspberry.

'Also, that was wrong. Really wrong to

wish for Dad to win the race.'

'Gah?' Birdie looked at her big sister.

Birdie didn't blow a raspberry this time. Flick wondered if this meant Birdie felt bad about what she'd done.

Well, she should feel bad. She'd ruined sports day. Right when Flick had been enjoying it so much. 'I'm taking you back to Mum and Dad,' Flick said. 'I'm tired of wishes. In fact, I wish there were no wishes. I wish there were no wishes at all.'

12

One more wish

Inside the tent, Flick's parents had spread out the picnic rug and set out their lunch.

Flick sat right on the edge of the rug. She wasn't hungry.

Birdie kept crawling across the rug towards Flick.

'Gah!' Birdie said, over and over again.

Flick turned away each time.

'I don't understand why you're so grumpy, Flick,' her dad said finally. 'Have you had enough water?'

'Yes,' Flick said grumpily. 'I've had enough water.' *And I've definitely had enough wishes,* she added in her head.

'Gah!' Birdie said, crawling over yet again. **'Gah, gah, gah.'**

'Flick,' Oli said. 'I think Birdie wants something.'

A whistle came from the stroller basket next to Flick.

'Ah, I see our friend the imp's back,' Flick's mum said.

Flick's head whipped around to look at her mum. What? She knew about the wishes now? Birdie must have unwished her wish!

'Gah!' Birdie said once more.

'Oli's right,' the imp said.

'About what?' Flick asked.

'About Birdie. She wants to tell you something.'

Flick sighed. 'I suppose she's sorry. About making Dad win the parent–teacher race.'

'Birdie didn't wish for your dad to win the race,' the imp said. 'That was just luck.'

Flick gave the imp a look.

'It's true! He won that race fair and square. Sometimes that's how races go. Anything can happen.'

Flick glanced briefly at her dad. 'I don't believe you. The wind. The bunting. The falling over. That was all … luck?' she said.

'Yep. A whole lot of luck!' the imp said.

There was a moment of shocked silence.

'Wow,' Oli said.

'Wow,' Flick said.

'It was a bit wow,' the imp agreed.

Flick looked at her little sister, then patted her lap. Birdie crawled in. 'Sorry, Birdie,' Flick said. 'I thought you'd wished for Dad to win.'

'Gah.' Birdie shook her head. Then she put a hand on Flick's arm. 'Gah,' she repeated.

Flick knew Birdie was saying sorry too.

She was sorry that she'd made their parents forget about the wishes.

'That's okay,' Flick said. She noticed that Birdie didn't have her special t-shirt on anymore either. And it was funny, but now that Flick knew their dad winning hadn't been a wish, she sort of missed that t-shirt.

Flick suddenly found she was starving. She asked her dad for a sandwich. He took Birdie from her and put her down on the rug. Then he passed Flick the box of sandwiches. As Flick ate, she thought about the wishes. And Granny Aggie. And Birdie. And herself.

'You've got a funny look on your face,'

said the imp. 'Is your sandwich bad? I'll have it.'

Flick passed the imp a sandwich. It liked sandwiches.

'Thanks.' The imp stuffed the whole sandwich in its mouth at once.

Flick laughed at the imp's puffy cheeks. 'I was just thinking. I can't wish because I'm not a baby. But Birdie won't be a baby for very long either. And then I guess the wishes will go away. Is that right?'

'Guess you'll have to wait and see,' the imp said, its mouth full.

Flick watched her little sister, who was laughing at the imp's chipmunk cheeks. Flick really did want to be the best big sister ever. A big part of that was protecting Birdie. But another part of it was having fun together. Thinking back, all of the wishes today had been pretty funny – Birdie becoming an air horn, Birdie turning green, even the bicycle legs … Birdie was doing okay with her wishes. Maybe Flick didn't need to worry quite so much.

'Imp?' Flick said.

'Whassup?' The imp was busy licking its sandwich fingers.

'If Birdie wished for something, could you help to make it a nice wish? No twisting?'

'Sorry. But twisting's fun.'

'Maybe you could make it a *nice* twist?' Oli suggested.

'Please?' Flick added.

The imp looked surprised. 'People don't usually say please.'

'They don't?' Flick said. 'That's a bit rude.'

'I know, right!'

Flick decided she'd give it a go. She leaned forwards and whispered in her sister's ear.

Birdie gazed up at her big sister and nodded. **'Gah, gah, gah,'** she said, making her wish.

'What is it?' Oli looked around. 'What did you wish for?'

And then the squeals started. Excited squeals.

Oli stood.

'Wait. Is that ...?' Oli was staring at something in the distance.

It was.

There was a snow cone truck driving across the sports field. Just like the one Oli had mentioned this morning.

The kids went wild.

Flick peered into the stroller basket again.

'What's the twist?' she asked the imp. Surely there would only be liquorice-flavoured snow cones. Or worse, worm-flavoured.

The imp grinned. 'The twist is there's only one flavour,' it said, looking proud of itself.

Flick sighed. She knew it. 'And what flavour's that?' she said nervously.

'Lime,' the imp said. 'There are only two races left. The green team can't be beaten. They're the winners of the sports day cup. Everyone can have green snow cones to celebrate! See? I can do nice twists when I feel like it.'

The end

Add these magical books to your wish list!

Allison Rushby made a wish when she was six years old. She wished to be a ballerina with pierced ears. Not long after this, she wrote her very first book (not about a ballerina) and decided to be an author with pierced ears instead. She went on to write many more books, for both adults and children, though none of them were sticky-taped together like that first one. She lives in Brisbane with her family and her two not very useful assistants, Harry the Bordoodle and Titus the Sphynx. To learn more about Allison, visit www.allisonrushby.com.

When **Karen Blair** was young she wished she could see the fairies in the garden and would sometimes leave baked beans out for them. She also wished that she could draw all day and now the wish has come true! Karen loves to illustrate characters that are young, old and in between. She lives in Fremantle, Western Australia, with her husband, two children and a small dog called Dobby, who thinks he's a cat. To learn more about Karen, visit www.karenblair.com.au.

First published 2023 by University of Queensland Press
PO Box 6042, St Lucia, Queensland 4067 Australia

University of Queensland Press (UQP) acknowledges the Traditional Owners and their custodianship of the lands on which UQP operates. We pay our respects to their Ancestors and their descendants, who continue cultural and spiritual connections to Country. We recognise their valuable contributions to Australian and global society.

uqp.com.au
reception@uqp.com.au

Cover design by Mika Tabata
Cover and internal illustrations by Karen Blair
Author photograph by Little Family Photo Co.
Illustrator photograph by Jessica Wyld
Typeset in 14.75/24 pt Minion Pro by UQP
Printed in Australia by McPherson's Printing Group

Australian Government | Australia Council for the Arts

University of Queensland Press is assisted by the Australian Government through the Australia Council, its arts funding and advisory body.

A catalogue record for this book is available from the National Library of Australia.

ISBN 978 0 7022 6594 5 (pbk)
ISBN 978 0 7022 6809 0 (epdf)
ISBN 978 0 7022 6810 6 (epub)

University of Queensland Press uses papers that are natural, renewable and recyclable products made from wood grown in well-managed forests and other controlled sources. The logging and manufacturing processes conform to the environmental regulations of the country of origin.

FSC www.fsc.org MIX Paper | Supporting responsible forestry FSC® C001695